The Card of the Month Club

The Card of the Month Club

...how a family tradition begins

A Memoir

Brenda Boyce

BBink
Bloomfield Hills, MI LLC

Published by

BB *ink*
Bloomfield Hills, MI LLC

Publisher's Cataloging-in-Publication Data
Boyce, Brenda.

The Card of the Month Club : how a family tradition begins : a memoir / Brenda Boyce. – Bloomfield Hills, MI : BB ink, 2012.

p. ; cm.

ISBN13: 978-0-9860194-0-1

1. Greeting cards. 2. Families. 3. Love. I. Title.

BJ2095.G5 B69 2012
395—dc23

FIRST EDITION

Project coordination by Jenkins Group, Inc.
www.BookPublishing.com

Illustrations by Annette Cable
Author photo by Boswell Creative Inc.
Interior design by Yvonne Fetig Roehler

Printed in the United States of America
16   15   14   13   12   •   5   4   3   2   1

For the members of
The Card of the Month Club

Helen Blake
Stan Boyce
Eleanor Boyce

*I*t was Christmas Eve, and I had no gift for my mother. The stores had been closed for hours, so I sat staring at a dying fire, willing myself to think. Upstairs, my mother slept, unaware that Santa's sack was empty.

Charred logs illuminated a large ficus tree near the fireplace, casting its shadow against the ceiling. Only three weeks before, while I'd been busy entwining miniature white Christmas lights among the branches, the telephone had rung. I'd piled the lights on a nearby chair, not knowing I would never pick them up again.

My son John had been in an accident, I was told, and his condition was grave.

Thirty minutes later, when the telephone rang again, the caller asked to speak to my husband.

"No," I said. "Whatever you have to say, you will say to me."

The pile of lights remained on that chair until the day of John's funeral, when my mother removed them, saying, "You won't need these now."

I stared at the fading glow of the embers and replayed my mother's words when she arrived the following morning to stay with me.

"This is the first day I am glad your father is no longer alive," she announced, "for there would have been two funerals this week if he had been told that John is dead."

My father's heart had failed only eighteen months before.

Bereaved anew at John's loss, a season of joy became a season of sorrow, and we removed a chair from our family's table for the second Christmas in a row.

As I watched the warmth and light of the fire die, I heard Mother stir upstairs. My thoughts turned to how often she had come to me during the night since John's death, when my grief was overwhelming.

She was gentle and strong, a cushion when I cried, but she would be returning home soon, and it weighed on me that she would be alone with her memories in an empty house.

I pictured my mother's small frame enveloped in my father's oversized chair, her toes barely touching the floor. I could see her sitting there every morning, as was her custom, waiting for her mail. She lived in a town so small that Bill, her mailman, not only opened the unlocked front door and brought the mail to her but also usually announced its contents.

"Helen," he might say as he handed over her delivery, "electric bills are out today. And you got a letter from Brenda."

Mother loved getting mail. She kept letters for weeks, reading them over and over. "It's like they're visiting again," she would say.

She waited for her mail in joyous expectation, never knowing what Bill would bring. For her, every morning was her birthday, and she so enjoyed sharing her correspondence with family and friends that I'd learned years ago not to write anything that I didn't want the neighbors to read.

My musings had carried me far into the night, and nothing remained of the fire but ashes. In the muted light of the streetlamp that lit the room, the white mantel stood in soft relief against the tenebrous hearth it bordered. As I studied the envelope-shaped fireplace, an idea began to form, and suddenly I knew what my mother's Christmas gift would be.

For the next twelve months, I would send my mother a card. It might arrive anytime during the month, but

never for any specific occasion. She could enjoy watching for her card every morning as she sat in my father's chair, the exclusive member of what I spontaneously dubbed the "The Card of the Month Club."

I pulled myself to my feet, searched my office, gathered calligraphy supplies and several yellowed sheets of parchment, and began writing.

Some time later, I signed the parchment document with a flourish, rolled it into a scroll, and tied a gold ribbon around the middle. I found an aluminum foil box for wrapping, but it was hardly worthy packaging. On a whim, I clipped the corners and glued the cardboard flat on a remnant of emerald green velvet in celebration of my mother's Irish heritage.

Reassembling the box, I wrapped my gift in a flowered silk scarf, using a photograph of my son and father in a warm embrace for the gift tag.

As Christmas Day dawned, I placed my present on the kitchen table.

"Such a pretty package," my mother commented as she entered the room. "What is it?"

"Actually, Mom, it's twelve gifts," I replied, "only you haven't received them yet."

She paused. "Then why did you wrap the box?"

Mother returned home in early January, and her first card of the month soon followed. In it, I included pressed flowers to match the cover illustration. A seashell from the Caribbean was enclosed with her

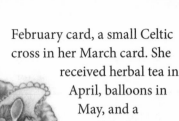

February card, a small Celtic cross in her March card. She received herbal tea in April, balloons in May, and a polished stone from Lake Superior in June.

My mother loved the cards, and left them on her sofa table for all to see.

I began to find that I could not pass a card or gift shop without wandering in, and once I explained my mission to the store's owner, we would usually begin exploring the store together. Other customers, drawn by our laughter, often asked me about the card of the month club.

"What a good idea," they would say. "I should do that, too." Then they would tell me their stories, and I came to realize that the card of the month club is not just for those who receive cards but also for those who need to send them.

I never signed Mother's cards with my name, only with the moniker I had given myself as president of the Card of the Month Club – The Prez. She could identify her card before it was opened, for the return address was always abbreviated C.O.T.M.C.

Bill began watching for her cards, and soon he could be heard calling out, "Your card of the month came today!"

My mother loved the cards, but by October, as it became more difficult to find entertaining enclosures to match a card's theme, I was counting the months until my promise would end. Once, I asked my mother which she liked more, the cards or the enclosures.

"What I like," she said, "is being remembered."

Later that fall, my father-in-law's health began to fail, and my husband and I feared his condition was terminal. We traveled east to spend Christmas with him, and I pondered what gift I could take to cheer him. My thoughts kept returning to one thing: another subscription to the Card of the Month Club. As I prepared a second scroll for my father-in-law, I began thinking of masculine enclosures he would enjoy.

On January 31, the phone rang. It was my mother.

"I didn't get my card of the month," she complained.

"You're not supposed to," I said. "That was last year's Christmas gift."

"I like my cards."

"Am I supposed to send you cards forever?"

A long silence ensued.

"I'm sending cards to Stan now, you know," I offered.

"Yes, but I still want my card of the month."

"Let me look into the club's subscription policy," I replied, "and I'll get back to you."

"Fine, but I want my cards."

That was that.

I prepared an official-looking memo from the circulation department of the Card of the Month Club. It stated that the president had received a complaint from one of the members about the club's strict subscription policy, suggesting that it wasn't too late to change her will. Thus, the president had revised the club's policy and was now offering members the following options:

☐ *Please cancel my subscription. Those cards are really dumb.*

☐ *Three-month trial subscription. I want nice cards this time.*

☐ *One-year subscription. Do I get a baker's dozen?*

☐ *Send cards until the cows come home.*

The memo asked each member to check a box and return the form to the club's circulation manager, Ima Sucker.

Both my mother and my father-in-law checked the last box and promptly returned their forms in the self-enclosed, stamped envelopes.

I was sending two cards each month now.

For my father-in-law, I enclosed his favorite candy, Werther's; a decal from his alma mater, Duke; a picture of his first car, a 1932 Ford Roadster; and a variety of jokes and cartoons.

Every card of the month was displayed on his desk, where it remained a source of conversation for visitors until his death nearly two years later.

As my husband and I were packing to return home following his funeral, my mother-in-law came to me. Taking my hand, she looked up at me with teary eyes and said, "I guess this means you won't be sending any more cards."

I hesitated. My mother and father-in-law were official members of the Card of the Month Club. My mother-in-law was not, but still...

"You know," I finally said, "I'm not exactly sure what estate provisions are in the Card of the Month Club subscription agreement."

"Why don't you ask Ima Sucker?" she sweetly replied.

My circulation manager's reply began with "Whereas," and continued with a declaration and articles lifted directly from my will, legal passages from old incorporation papers, high school Latin phrases, Chinese greetings, and French cooking terms.

Ima Sucker concluded that the very fine print – some might say so fine as to be invisible – of the club's original agreement stated that my mother-in-law, Eleanor, could inherit her husband's subscription to the Card of the Month Club.

I stapled construction paper across the top of the memo in the manner of legal documents and shipped the finding to my mother-in-law.

Delighted, she called me immediately.

"I'm not sure I understand all the legal terms," she told me, "but that Ima Sucker really knows her law."

I was back to sending two cards each month.

Since my husband Tom was traveling abroad regularly now, it was time for the Card of the Month Club to go international. I gave him cards to mail from foreign lands and he added local souvenirs and always affixed large colorful stamps, even when it was too much postage.

Our mothers received silk scarves from Shanghai, origami birds from Tokyo, and incense from Bangkok. Their cards of the month from Kuala Lumpur, the pewter capitol of the world, included pewter medallions. Linen handkerchiefs edged with Belgian lace found their way from Brussels, tiny spoons arrived from Dusseldorf, and small leather purses journeyed from Florence. Saffron from Barcelona, lavender from Dubrovnik, coffee beans from Sao Paulo, and spices from Mumbai spilled out of their cards. For ten years, until his retirement, Tom carried a unique card of the month for each of our mothers everywhere he went.

When my mother could no longer live at home alone, I moved her closer to me. She lived in various assisted-living communities and finally a nursing home. Wherever she lived, her card of the month followed. The card was always mailed, even though I visited her nearly every day. More than once, I was present when her card arrived. Parkinson's disease and two strokes left her nearly paralyzed the last months of her life, but I could still see her smile when one of her aides would say, "Helen, your card of the month came today."

On the morning of her sixty-seventh wedding anniversary, a grey Saturday in November, my mother's breathing became irregular. With a soft sigh, she was gone. Her nurse covered her with a crocheted throw and quietly slipped away, leaving me alone with my mother. I held her still-warm hand and looked around the room. On the bedside table stood her last card of the month, with a photograph of her twin great-grandchildren celebrating their first birthdays.

I stood in dim light, remembering the Christmas Eve when I'd taken out a yellowed piece of parchment and penned a promise that would become the Card of the Month Club. Smiling, I thought of my mother gleefully returning her subscription form to Ima Sucker and the joy the cards had brought her. Seventeen years had passed since that Christmas Eve, and now my mother's once exclusive membership in the Card of the Month Club would belong to my mother-in-law. The cows had finally come home.

I leaned over to kiss my mother goodbye as attendants wheeled a gurney into her room. I could see a zippered body bag folded neatly on top. It was emerald green velvet.

Acknowledgments

FOR TOM, who helped me live the story.

FOR MY FELLOW WRITERS, who encouraged me to tell the story.

FOR ALETTE AND TODD, who designed my logo to share the story.

FOR LINDA AND DICK, who offered their prayers in support of the story.

FOR JAMIE AND SPENCER, who celebrated their first birthdays in the story.

And FOR LILLI, who sat in her dog bed on my desk and licked my nose while I was writing the story.

You are my family, too.